After Krato enemies destroy their world, Lasarian refugees flee through the veil hidden in the Soul Mirror and find a haven on Earth.

After decades of peace with the native humans, fear and jealousy has created a dangerous world for the Lasarian people, and they now live a hunt or be hunted existence.

Danek Kavarac resolves to endure the pain of the loss of his soulmate. Life must go on—until he meets Amari Vaselka, next in line to the crown. A woman that he cannot escape. A woman who can heal his soul. Now he must become the man she deserves or die trying.

Soul Mirror
Copyright © 2023 Remi Auguste
ISBN: 978-1-4874-3743-5
Cover art by Martine Jardin

Published by eXtasy Books Inc.

Look for us online at:
www.eXtasybooks.com

Soul Mirror
Omega Rys Series 1

By

Remi Auguste

PROLOGUE

The balcony railing shook under Queen Arrah's hands as a rocket slammed into the planet, sending dust and debris soaring into the air. Trees burned on the horizon, their flames leaping, resembling angry fingers. The seconds felt like ages as the battle for the Lasarian home world raged before her. The high-pitched whine of a Kratoan warship reached Arrah's ears. She pulled the hood of her cloak back and peered up at the clouds as the shadow of the hulking spaceship came into view. Her heart pounded as she watched it descend to the capital city.

Arrah feared Lasaria had fallen.

The Kratoan savages had come three nights before, systematically ravaging her small planet and entering the capital city that morning. She had been jarred awake earlier by the echoes of laser fire and explosions that rocked the walls of her bedroom.

Arrah retreated to the safety of the throne room, closing the balcony doors tightly behind her. Her boots crunched on shards of glass as she crossed the room, each step feeling like the last time she would walk this route. The slivers of shattered mirrors on the polished wooden floor reflected a distorted image of her disheveled appearance and echoed the fall of Lasaria.

She took a moment to glance around the room. Broad white marble columns supported the roof high above her. Tapestries in a myriad of colors and designs hung on the walls surrounding her, each paying tribute to a queen of the past. She stopped in front of her favorite, her gaze traveling over her mother's tapestry. Queen Kosa was born in the year of the flower harvest, and her tapestry reflected an ornate floral pattern woven with the finest threads of purple and silver. Her mother had died suddenly only months earlier, leaving Arrah as the youngest queen to rule Lasaria.

Arrah had stood in the same spot countless times since she was a girl, in awe of each handwoven stitch. She could still hear the shrill of her mother's warnings, *Don't touch the art, Arrah.* She hadn't gotten around to adding her own contribution to the walls. Her tapestry would have hung next to her mother's. It didn't matter now. She suspected that this room, her home, would be in ruins within days.

She reached out and ran her hand over the stitches, then gripped it with both hands and yanked it down. The Kratoans were not going to take everything from her. She hugged the heavy tapestry to her chest, pulled it off the floor, then proceeded to the end of the room and sat on her throne.

Her mate was out there somewhere with her people, and she hadn't received a message from him in two days. She cast an anxious look toward the throne room doors, hoping for news of his safety.

She was Lasarian, a race existing in the Omega Rys Galaxy. Her soul was connected to the elements, the spirit of life, and her mate. With training, Lasarians could manipulate the world around them. They called these abilities Magiks.

Long ago, their ruling deity was the Goddess Arlaya. When she had walked among her people, she contained all Magiks in her blood. As her children grew in numbers and prospered, their Magik became diluted, with each being having power over only one type. Lasarian Magiks passed down through bloodlines, spirit healers being the most revered clans. The ability to heal was a rare Magik. As reigning queen, Arrah was the last with healing Magik. Legends held that queens had once been able to restore life.

Lasarians weren't war folk and were wary of other species and worlds. Kratoan raids and attacks targeted Lasarians as objects used only for their powers. A weakened Lasarian had no control over their Magik, making it vulnerable to being siphoned for use by the enemy.

Arrah recalled chilling tales of her people being captured and tortured, then laid out on barren fields to bring life back into the soil. Others told stories of healers being kept in display cases to be touched when someone needed healing of illness or injury. She shivered and clutched the tapestry closer. She wasn't about to let that happen to her.

Arrah closed her eyes, thoughts of survival circling through her mind. She said a quiet prayer in her heart that her people would survive to see another day. She knew their last resort was to abandon Lasaria through the spatial veil to another world. Her gaze rested on the only mirror still mounted to the wall on her right. Even to the unsuspecting eye, this wasn't an ordinary mirror. The glass was the darkest black, with edges that refracted the light into rainbows.

Ancient Lasarians with Glass Magik had created mirrors with materials harvested from their land, then imbued them with a sliver of their soul to create portals. They called them Soul Mirrors. The one next to her was one of only a handful of these portals still in functioning condition.

The Kratoan enemies were ruthless and capable of shapeshifting. They didn't bother hiding their fierce natural form as they ransacked Lasaria. They were a race of eight-foot-tall beasts with biologically armored flesh. Their energies were dark and black, suffocating the land.

Arrah folded the tapestry in her lap and tucked it into the large bag at her feet, which held her mother's healing crystals, sacred writings and spells, and other personal items she didn't want to lose. She settled the thick leather strap over her

3

shoulder and went to stand before the Soul Mirror. Her blue eyes stared back at her. Long waves of platinum blonde hair hung down her back, tousled by stress and fitful sleep. She had dressed in a royal blue battle dress and a hooded cloak, firmly secured at her slender throat. Her leather boots came up to her thighs, and she had secured her blade in the scabbard at her back.

Arrah sensed her mate's spirit getting close and released a deep sigh of relief, his essence bringing some peace to her restless soul.

His footsteps thundered from the hall, coming closer to her haven, and she assumed a stance ready to defend herself if trouble followed him. Her palm closed around the blade's hilt at her back. The ornate double doors crashed open, and she relaxed at seeing her mate standing in the doorway.

Kiell's wet, sweaty hair clung to his face, his chest heaving beneath his bloodied shirt that hung in tatters. His gaze found hers, the wild look on his face shifting to one of resolve. He slammed the doors shut and bolted them before turning back to her. His black and white cloak billowed around him as he crossed the room in large strides. He took her into his arms, held her close, and briefly buried his face in her hair.

She leaned into his embrace and inhaled the stench of blood, sweat, and soot.

The smell of war.

"Arrah, we need to leave. Now!" Kiell urged her toward the mirror.

"Is there anyone else?" Arrah peered over his shoulder toward the doors, hopeful for survivors.

His arms tightened around her and spoke softly in her ear. "I sent many of our people through the veil. We'll gather them on the other side. I'm sorry, Arrah, but the Kratoans are coming, and I couldn't risk not being able to come back for you and our child." He rested his hand on her swollen belly, placing a loving kiss on her head while keeping her within the safety of his embrace.

A bright flash from the balcony doors caught Arrah's attention. Another Kratoan rocket plummeted from the heavens and exploded into the city. Their home shook beneath their feet. Kiell steadied her and shielded her body with his own as stones and dust crashed around them. Tears burned Arrah's eyes as the destruction of her palace intensified.

"I'm sorry, honey," Kiell murmured against her hair. "I promise I'll find a safe place for our family."

His hand was warm in hers as he pulled her closer to the Soul Mirror. Kiell's words reminded her that this building didn't make up the roots of her people. All that mattered right now was their love and their unborn child. Arrah was confident that they could make a home anywhere.

They stood mere inches from the Mirror as her mate began the incantation to activate the veil. His voice carried a different lilt as he brought the Magik forth from his soul.

Kiell circled his hand over the center of his chest, gathering energy until a white shimmer surrounded him, then pressed his palm against the black glass. The portal recognized Kiell's soul, and the shield fell, the molecules in the glass shifting to allow passage.

Arrah squeezed her mate's hand tight as they fled through the veil to a new world.

CHAPTER ONE

Four, five, six… Fuck. Danek's gaze shifted from human to human, his eyes watering from the smoky haze in the bar. He stopped counting, growing wary of the number of hunters in his place of business. Human hunters gathered only when planning something big. It was still well before midnight, plenty of time for an attack — the question of when and where was what plagued him. He forced his attention away from the crowd and concentrated on buffing the watermarks off the glass in his hands.

Adriel, co-owner of *Villa*, his partner in crime and friend, must have noticed his unease. "Easy, D. Nothing's going down before the sun sets. They're probably just scoping out the hottest bar on Earth."

Danek briefly glanced at him and snorted. Adriel was acting casual, but he also seemed somewhat wary.

Danek took a deep breath, inhaling the scent of the wood and musk of his bar, then focused on his task. He turned to stack the spotless glass on the shelf with the rest. He stepped back to admire the shelves in the middle of the wall behind the bar filled with sparkling crystalline glassware. Each level contained specialized glasses for specific drinks. On the bottom were the ones for ale, beer, and pilsners, followed by low-balls, highballs, and mixers. Dangling neatly from the next was various stemware for wines and cocktails, and the final level held the sparkling crystal shot glasses. All of them were pristine.

Danek took a moment to appreciate how the light entered

each glass, refracted, and came out changed. It was something he could always see with his gift of Glass Magik. Atoms in glass recognized him, came alive in his hands, and he could manipulate them into whatever shape he desired. As a Glasser, he could produce heat in his hands, making them capable of creating glass from its most basic components.

Danek's thoughts drifted to his parents. His father had been a Glasser, too, and his family had served the royal family on Lasaria for eons. The Kratoans had executed his father during the Dark War, and his mother had fled to Earth with her newborn baby — him — and the other refugees.

The Lasarians had initially found peace and refuge among Earthlings since their anatomy closely resembled humans and blended in well. For the first couple of decades on Earth, they lived in harmony forming small communities. The rural town of Toska became a central hub for many Lasarian refugees, and the town's human population welcomed the Lasarians' use of their Magik to support crops, improve the production of resources, and heal the sick.

When the town began to grow, politicians and people of power began to resent and fear the Lasarians' superior abilities. Campaigns for slandering Lasarians spread throughout Toska, encouraging humans to reject the aliens and kill them on sight.

Humans were physically weaker than most Lasarians but were still a threat Danek preferred not to have behind every corner. The human hunters were getting brave, coming out in plain view.

The familiar scent of the soap Adriel was using to wash the dirty glasses drifted to his nostrils. Suddenly, a warm heat washed over him, replacing the smell — not from the air, but from a *soul*.

He swiveled and saw two females stroll into the bar. They quickly pulled out chairs, laughing and parking themselves at a table. Trying not to be too obvious, he scrutinized them, scanning them from head to toe. Using his sixth sense allowed him to visualize the emotions of living beings as energy reflecting their soul. It was an energy that could transfer from one to the other for specific purposes or unintentionally.

A Lasarian's soul fueled their Magik. The stronger the soul, the more control they had over their energy. If it was not well controlled, it drifted freely from the host and influenced the emotions of others in their proximity. Danek had been taught from a very young age how to shield his mind to prevent influence from other souls. He had also learned that a mate could sense a change in their counterpart's energy at any distance.

A mate?

Nearly five years before, he'd had a mate, Eela, who was his pride and joy, and life had been beautiful, happy. Her lovely face framed by shiny black hair that she wore in thick braids still haunted him day and night, her midnight blue eyes that sparkled with love, her melodious voice… He still longed to hear her, smell her fragrance, and touch her satiny skin, to have her in his arms at night. His soul remained tormented by guilt.

He should have taken every opportunity to be by her side instead of putting his rank in the military first. He had been a captain in the Lasarian military, the Sirak, and home on leave. He and Eela were planning dinner and a shopping trip when the chieftain ordered him to report back to duty for an urgent mission. There was no time and no other choice for him.

Danek's world fell apart the day he received the news that his wife had gone to the market alone and never returned. He left his post and rushed home to help in the search. The Lasarian guard spent months investigating. When they finally found her, it was too late. She died in his arms on the coldest, darkest night of his life.

Eela's death changed him. The memory of her both

tortured him and kept him safe from falling in love with someone else. He wasn't certain he could handle the loss of another woman. He had purposely walled off his heart and soul and stayed away from females.

Snapping out of his self-pity mode, he gazed at the two Lasarian females seated at the table. One of them was calling to his soul. The petite brunette had a blended auburn and yellow aura, signifying her as a mated female. She tossed her hair and gazed around the bar. Could it be the blonde? Her aura was cerulean blue, and he felt emotions that were not his own penetrating his barriers. He followed the curve of her breasts down to her curvy little belly and felt something stirring within, something he had not experienced for a very long time.

Danek's attention snapped away from the stunning female when Adriel stormed out from behind the bar and crossed the short distance to where the blonde sat. He could see the muscle in Adriel's jaw twitch as he spoke to the woman, who had risen to her feet when he approached. Adriel grabbed her arm as she shrugged off her jacket. The supple brown leather slid off her toned bicep, and Danek got a good look at the cascade of floral lace tattooed down her arm. His libido stirred, but he forced it down deep. Instead, his temper shifted to aggression at seeing Adriel's forceful hand on her. Adriel was tall and burly, but she jerked her arm away and stood nose-to-nose with him.

Danek noticed a pink flush creeping up her neck as they argued. Her cerulean blue spirit matched Adriel's and clashed together so dangerously that they would soon get out of control, affecting the humans around them, causing them to become violent and angry.

Danek set down the glass he'd been polishing and left the bar. He weaved through the tables toward the arguing pair. While he walked, he surveyed the room, now dimly lit by the last rays of the sun. He sensed the hunters, who had pushed two tables together and were sipping their beers. So far, they hadn't ordered more than two, so they were still half-decently sober. His alert mode was still in high gear, but he didn't feel an immediate threat coming from their direction.

"Is there a problem here, Adriel?" Danek was determined to diffuse the situation and get a closer look at the woman. He spread his legs, crossed his arms, and focused on her. The female turned her crystal-blue eyes on him and imitated his stance, indicating she knew who was in charge. And it was neither he nor Adriel.

"Who are you?" she asked in a blasé tone.

Danek bowed slightly. "Danek Kavarac, at your service."

With a slight toss of her hair, she dismissed him.

He presumed it was because she'd either never heard of him or that she had and just didn't care.

Adriel straightened even taller and sighed. "Danek, please allow me to reacquaint you with my sister, Amari."

"Twin sister," she corrected, scowling at her brother, "but so much more powerful."

"I don't doubt your power, darling," Danek said, earning a radiant smile from her, a smile that somehow touched his heart.

Adriel and Amari's mother was Queen Arrah. Danek had met her once, and her presence had been powerful and memorable. Maybe that was why he could feel this female so strongly. His gaze lingered on her face. Faint recognition fluttered through his brain. They had been kids when they'd last seen each other, and Amari hardly resembled the little girl he once knew. He'd heard she'd gone away to a human university.

"My friend insisted on coming to Villa tonight to celebrate my homecoming since my brother didn't even bother to pick me up from the train station." Amari narrowed her eyes in

Adriel's direction, then gave Danek a sidelong glance as she continued. "It's too loud and crowded in here for my taste. I doubt we will stay long."

Danek raised his brows. "May I welcome you home? Drinks on the house if you'll stay. I'm honored that you came out to my place."

Amari's expression softened, and she stepped closer to him, resting her warm hand on his cheek.

"Danek." She stared into his eyes. "It's been literal ages since I've seen you. Sure, I'll stay for a drink or two. Maybe even a dance."

Adriel rolled his eyes. "Amari, just take your friend elsewhere. Preferably home. This is no place for you."

"She'll be fine, Adriel. We're here to keep her safe." Danek tried to pacify his friend.

"Relax, brother. Let me have a drink and settle back in my hometown. I promise to leave before anything *fun* happens."

"And by fun, you mean finding someone too loud, so you feel like knocking them down a few pegs. Honestly, Ree. Do *not* start a fight tonight. Especially here." After his warning, Adriel stalked away, leaving Danek with Amari. The swinging door to the bar smacked so hard against it that an olive bounced out of the garnish tray.

Danek cleared his throat. "What can I bring you, ladies?"

Amari shoved a few curls away from her face and sat down with her friend, obviously unphased by Adriel's tantrum. Her gaze settled on his face, and her lips curved into a beautiful smile.

"I felt your energy shift when you remembered me. I'm embarrassed I didn't recognize my favorite Glasser. I'm sorry." Amari apologized.

As a personal rule, Danek kept his energy behind strong mental barriers. No one had been able to cross them and access his soul in a long time. What Magik did this woman possess that allowed her to bypass his shield?

"No worries, honey. Now, what can I get for you?"

Her friend shoved her arm and whispered, but his keen hearing picked up what she said.

"You know what I've heard about Glassers?"

Amari shoved her back and smiled.

Danek shifted his stance because he knew what the woman was alluding to. The blush on her cheeks was a dead giveaway and quite amusing. Glassers had a reputation for their ability to sexually please a woman beyond any other. The heat of a Glasser's hands brought their body to intense sensual levels that females found intoxicating.

Two pairs of eyes focused on him, now assessing him openly and throwing him flirtatious looks.

"Let me bring you ladies something tall and refreshing to cool you down." He surprised himself with his flirtatious tone. For the first time in years, a woman had a profound effect on him.

Amari studied him for a moment, a curious expression in her eyes. "Cosmopolitan times two, please."

Danek gave her a wide grin. She seemed to be relaxing. He walked back to the bar to mix the drinks, contemplating whether he should knock down the walls he'd built around his heart.

Was it finally time?

CHAPTER TWO

Danek busied himself behind the bar pouring drinks and serving meals. Restless thoughts from his past continued to course through his mind.

Adriel clapped him on the shoulder, jarring his mind back to the present. "You been watching the game? We're winning."

Danek glanced up at the television mounted in the corner. He didn't really care about the football game flashing across the screen.

"D, you've been polishing that glass for twenty minutes. What's going on?" Adriel leaned on the bar and crossed his arms, concern written on his face.

Danek looked down at the glass in his hands. "Got a lot on my mind tonight." He forced a smile and put the glass down. His gaze wandered over the crowd and lingered when he located Amari on the dance floor. The woman was breathtaking.

The thumping bass and flashing lights dulled as he admired the sight of her body moving to the rhythm of the music. Her skin-tight golden dress rode up on her thigh while she danced with her friend in the throng of partiers. She threw her hair back, said something to her friend, and made her way back to her table. Her lips hypnotized him by how they curved against the glass as she drank the pink liquid, as did the dance of her curls on her curvy bottom when she swung her head back to take the last swallow. His gaze traced her hip and down her thigh, imagining how her skin would taste. She turned on her heels and approached the bar.

"Are you okay? Why not go out and get some air?" Adriel interrupted his thoughts again. "Amari is too relaxed. She's letting her energy drift too far. We're not zoned for an orgy."

Danek blinked hard, getting his senses under control. He shifted and adjusted the crotch of his jeans, which were getting uncomfortably tight, as he watched Amari sway up to the bar.

Amari wiggled between two patrons on barstools, earning displeased glares from them, and propped her elbows on the bar. "Can I get a cucumber water?"

Danek placed a square napkin in front of her and smiled broadly. "You bet, hon." He poured her drink from the frosty pitcher of infused water and placed it in front of her.

Amari's gaze found and held his while she took a long drink of her water. She set her glass down and cocked her head slightly to one side, her lips forming a perfect smile. "I'm actually having a really great time. I like what you've done with the place."

Danek's eyebrows rose in surprise. "I'm glad you're enjoying yourself. You deserve it."

He turned from her and moved down the bar, untying his apron as he walked. "I'm gonna step out for a minute," he muttered to Adriel as he passed his friend. He needed to relieve himself of his hard-on. Cool air and distancing himself from Amari should help.

Danek shoved the back door, propped it open with a brick, and stepped into the alleyway, taking a deep breath of November air. He peeled his t-shirt off, desperate to cool down and breathe. He lit a cigarette, took a long drag, and looked up at the sky littered with stars. His energy tensed around him when he sensed Amari's energy approaching.

"What are you doing out here, darlin'?" Amari's sultry voice called his attention away from the heavens.

He sighed. So much for distancing...

"Breathing." He fixed his gaze on the goddess ruffling his feathers. "It's crowded and hot in there."

Her gaze traced every muscle of his body and momentarily focused on his tell-tale crotch. "It looks like it's even hotter out here."

Danek tossed his smoke and locked gazes with her. Feeling her emotions set off an onslaught of his own, making it difficult to think clearly. "You're dangerously close to driving me mad, and you know it. You're lucky there aren't more Lasarians in attendance tonight, or you'd be in trouble. You're throwing around enough pheromones to drive someone weaker right into traffic."

Amari gave a very unladylike snort. "I can handle a room full of admirers." She slipped into her jacket. "It's the heat radiating from you that's making it hard for me to breathe."

His cock jerked in his jeans as he watched the leather slide over her skin. Resisting her took a great deal of effort. He knew who she was and had no business getting involved with a female of her status. He was damaged goods and did not need to saddle a woman with his baggage.

His species did not respect him. His reputation was that of a weak male for deserting his military post to search for his wife and being declared unfit to return to duty because of his debilitating grief.

Amari was a headache he did not want, but she stepped closer, staring at him with those blue eyes. She smelled so damn good. The mere scent of her did funny things to his brain. Her hand covered her mouth as she tried to stifle a yawn.

"Do you want me to drive you home, Princess?" He let his gaze wander over her, imagining her sitting in the seat next to him, her hand with those French-tipped nails resting on his thigh.

He raised his eyebrows as he noted her quickened breaths and the heat radiating from her. He couldn't quite make out what she wanted from him, but she was damned tempting.

"I'd love that, Danek. I don't think my friend will be ready to go for a while. Let me grab my bag and pay my tab." She smiled and disappeared back inside.

He stuck his head around the corner and called out to Adriel, "I have to take off for half an hour. Be back soon."

He grabbed his shirt from the crate, tugged it on, and walked to his 1968 Fathom Blue Chevelle. Empty soda bottles and wrappers lay scattered on the floor, and the interior didn't smell that great. He grabbed an empty shopping bag balled up in the glove box and quickly crammed the trash inside, stashing it behind the seat. Then he rummaged through the console, finding an old aerosol deodorant, and spritzing it throughout the cabin. He rolled the windows down to let in some fresh air.

Danek fired up the engine and tapped the gas, kicking off the choke, then pulled up to the door and waited for his passenger. He absently ran his fingers through his hair and leaned back against the seat, feeling more in control now that he sat behind the wheel of his car.

The back door of the bar opened several minutes later, and Amari stormed out, hollering. Adriel followed her out, yelling back at her.

She turned to face her brother. "You're my brother, not my father, Adriel." The pitch of her voice toned down some.

"You wouldn't listen to him either!" Adriel still sounded enraged. "You can't just run off with every Tom, Dick, or Harry! What happened to not needing a man?" Adriel shot a pointed look at Danek.

Danek considered whether to get involved in the sibling squabble but decided to sit tight for a little bit longer. Amari seemed to be holding her own.

"I don't need a man, Adriel." Amari cast her pretty gaze toward him. "He needs me."

Adriel stared at her for another moment, cast a dirty look in Danek's direction, then turned on his heel and went back inside the bar without another word.

Amari adjusted her purse strap on her shoulder and settled herself into the passenger seat. She flashed him a delicate smile. "Thanks for doing this. I'm kind of over this night." She rattled off the directions to her house.

Danek put his car in gear and pulled out of the alleyway, careful to drive easy with his precious passenger.

Silence reigned between them for the first few miles — Amari gazing out the passenger window while he watched the road. He checked the clock on the dash, determining it would be about a fifteen-minute drive to her place. He took his foot off the gas, slowing down to the speed limit.

The heated energy from Amari was cascading over him in waves. He sensed her restlessness. The empathic nature of the Lasarian people was either a great benefit or a torturous curse. He was leaning toward the latter.

The thoughts roiling in his brain demanded acknowledgment, so he broke the silence. "Look, Highness, I'm not in the market for a mate. It's not me that you want. If you're looking for a quick fuck, I can satisfy you, but there's someone better suited for you than me." He focused on the road and gripped the wheel tighter, waiting for her response.

She stilled as only Lasarians could. Her energy, breath, heartbeat, mind, and body froze. He glanced over at her, curious at the cessation of emotion.

Her voice purred soft and gentle when she spoke. "I'll keep better control of my energy if it's bothering you. I'm sorry for whoever you've lost. I want to help your spirit heal, if you'll let me."

He hadn't considered that she might be feeling *his* soul,

17

that perhaps she was also struggling with their unexpected attraction. His focus had been selfishly on what she was doing to *him*. She would have felt the guilt, sorrow, loneliness, and hell, the sheer panic he kept in the pit of his soul. And she still sought him out. What was wrong with this woman?

He followed her directions and pulled into her driveway too soon for his liking. The floodlight above her garage flicked on, sensing the motion. He shifted his car into park and sat back, turning to look at her.

She turned to face him and tucked her hair behind her ear. Shadows danced across her face as their connection sizzled between them. His brain spun, because she shouldn't be able to exchange emotions with him, but he could tell she sensed his grief and pain. The signs were there, but there was no way he could ever be her mate.

He kept his gaze locked with Amari's, just breathing. Being close to her, so near her body, set his soul on fire. His pain, rage, and guilt from his mate's death simmered near the surface, but his shields were meaningless when he was near her.

Amari took a deep breath. "Look, I feel something between us. I don't know if we should act on it or not. But let me do something for you."

He sighed deeply and got out of the car, pausing before opening the door for her. Lord help him, he wanted to go with her and let her fix him. Somewhere deep and dark in his soul lived the concern he wouldn't know who he was without the pain. Maybe he liked it. He took a deep breath at his heart's betrayal and opened her door.

She stood close to him and slid her hand up his arm. "Let me help, even if just for tonight."

She could do that. She could take control. She would be queen someday, and he was at her mercy.

He tried to focus on the chain hanging on his rearview mirror that had belonged to his Eela, a reminder of all he had lost.

Amari's hand on him was a cooling balm, soothing his soul and making him feel something good for a change.

He felt Amari feeding him energy, mending the frayed edges of his soul. "I feel you," he acknowledged in a whisper.

She moved closer and spoke to him gently. "You've been burning for so long, Danek. You don't have to forget, but I can take the hurt away."

He tried to hold onto the familiar pain, but she felt too damn good. He swallowed the lump in his throat and murmured, "Help me."

Time slipped away, the world blurred, and all that existed was her. He felt her fingers in his hair, pulling his head close to hers, and he let her. Her lips met his with a slow sensual kiss, then slipped over his bottom lip seductively as she continued pushing more healing energy into his soul. He moaned into her mouth and deepened the kiss.

"You are not damaged beyond repair," she whispered against his lips, kissed him once more, and stepped back. "Do you feel better?"

He stared into her bright blue eyes. Using her healing power caused the color to consume the white. Lasarian eyes were the one physical feature that distinguished them from humans, and he was lost in hers, speechless.

Amari smiled and touched his cheek. "Thanks for the ride. Let me give you my number." She held out her hand expectantly.

He hesitated a moment before realizing she was waiting for his phone. He swiped his unlock pattern and handed it to her without a second thought. She typed in some numbers and gave the phone back.

"I'm sure I'll see you soon. Be well," Amari said.

Danek got in his car and watched her walk up the sidewalk, unlock her door, and disappear into her house before he drove away. He felt peaceful with a clear mind. Great.

Clear enough to be occupied with figuring out what to do about Amari Vaselka. Her healing differed from the treatments the queen had forced upon him after Eela's death.

He had been distraught, violent, and destructive in his grief. The queen's healing had left him feeling sedated. Amari's healing felt as though she had woven part of herself into him. His soul felt resilient and less charred than it had been. He had thought he was stronger to carry the pain with him. But now he was ashamed of his weakness for refusing to put in the effort to be healed.

Danek drove back to the bar, wondering if Amari saw him as a patient or a lover. He suspected her mother, the queen, wouldn't be pleased if it was the latter.

CHAPTER THREE

Danek pocketed his keys as he entered through the bar's back door. Adriel was putting glasses of water down in front of a couple and returned their credit card.

"Last call!" Adriel hollered across the bar.

The DJ was packing up. The place had mostly emptied except for the hunters and a couple at the end of the bar.

Adriel glanced up at him briefly from restocking the wine fridge. "It's almost closing time."

"Sorry." Danek stretched his neck, apologetic that he'd been gone so long.

"What did Amari have to say to you?" Adriel asked.

Danek wiped down the bar. "Not a lot." He wasn't lying, since she hadn't said too much with her voice.

"I warned her not to mess with you. Did you just drop her off?" Adriel pried.

"I didn't go in, don't worry." Danek wrung out his towel and turned to look at his friend. "Would there be a problem with me dating your sister?"

Adriel's face showed his concern. He sighed. "Yes, I have a problem with it. It's no secret that you carry a heavy burden, D. Amari is very codependent. She is attracted to people she feels need her help and then gives it. Sometimes she has no business getting involved and trying to fix other people. It doesn't usually end well. I don't want you or her to come out of this worse than before."

Danek considered Adriel's words. He didn't know much about Amari's codependence but didn't want her to hurt because of it. He knew that a mated pair had to have compatible souls to bear strong, viable offspring. Magik use weakened the body, and mates were able to revitalize each other to an extent. The queen—as Amari was slated to become—required a man who could restore her with energy when she healed the sick and injured. She needed a soulmate. Amari deserved a soulmate.

Adriel throwing Danek's past in his face pissed him off. Everyone was acutely aware that he still held onto the memory of his deceased wife. He did so intentionally. Now, for the first time in years when he had considered letting her go, he risked his friendship with Adriel.

When the remaining patrons finished their drinks and left Danek turned the lock on the front door. "Do you think it's odd that the hunters didn't make a scene?"

Adriel shrugged. "Maybe Amari did us a favor. She threw around a decent amount of power tonight. Feeding off her influence, I bet they went home happy and horny."

"She definitely has a special kind of power," Danek murmured as he shrugged into his jacket. It bothered him that he wasn't sure where he stood with Amari, a woman who had turned his mind upside down within a few hours.

Adriel closed the register and gave Danek his full attention. "What's going on? You sure you're all right? You been quiet and distracted all night."

"Yeah, I'm fine." Danek just wanted to go home and get some sleep. He was anxious to relax and let his brain mull over his future. Maybe he could sleep a few hours without the chronic nightmares.

Adriel followed him out the back door and locked it behind them. "Okay... I guess I'll see you later." He walked down the alley and turned the corner toward the side lot where he always parked his car.

Danek reached in his pocket for his keys, settled himself

behind the wheel of his car, started it, then pulled out of the alley onto the main road. He glanced at the bar as he drove by out of habit, just to be sure his investment was tucked in safe for the night. Strange... Adriel's truck was still in the lot, but the driver's door was hanging open. Danek turned into the driveway and parked behind the vehicle, curious if his friend had forgotten his keys or something.

Adriel's booted feet hung from the driver's seat, indicating something was terribly wrong.

Danek's muscles tensed with dread, and his brain blared alarms. He remembered missions like this from his time in the Sirak military. He grabbed his knife from the glovebox and tucked it into his boot. His gaze scanned the tree line, suspecting the human hunters hadn't gone home as he and Adriel had thought. He opened his door and got out, and quickly sank to one knee.

"Adriel!" he called out, but his friend didn't move.

Danek did another quick scan of his surroundings before dashing over to Adriel. His friend was lying face down awkwardly over the console with an apparent gunshot to his back, a dark stain spreading on the right lower side.

"Adriel!" Danek tried again to bring his friend around. He leaned in, pressing two fingers to the pulse point of Adriel's throat, finding a rapid thready pulse.

Adriel gasped and groaned. "What the hell hit me?"

"Someone shot you. Looks pretty bad. We're gonna get outta here and get you some help."

The sound of a gunshot pierced the air and slammed into the truck door Danek was crouched behind.

"Fucking hell," he muttered. They were in a vulnerable situation, but his field training came flooding back, and he devised a quick plan to get them out alive. "Where're your keys, brother?"

Danek checked Adriel's pockets, felt underneath him, and

finally spied the keys on the floor. He ducked low as more bullets shattered the window, lodging into the seat cushions. He jammed the keys into the ignition, and the truck rumbled to life.

"Buddy, you're gonna need to move over. We're under fire, and this is gonna happen quickly," Danek warned.

Adriel grunted.

Danek interpreted that as consent and slipped his arm under Adriel's legs. "On the count of three... One... Two... Three!" Danek braced his feet and heaved his friend's body over the console into the other seat, and Adriel ended up slumped against the passenger door, half on the seat and half on the floor.

Gunfire peppered the truck as Danek jumped behind the wheel, crouched as low as he could, pulled the door shut, and threw the truck into drive. He slammed his foot down on the gas and peeled out of the lot, sending gravel and dust flying as he sped away.

"Damnit." Adriel wheezed. "How did I not see that coming?"

Danek cast a quick glance at Adriel, who hadn't moved. His breathing sounded ragged. "I'll get you to the queen."

"No," Adriel whispered. "Call...Amari. Won't make it...to Mom. Hurry."

"I got you. Stay with me." Danek checked the street signs, pulled a sharp right, and gunned the engine.

Adriel's energy was weak, and he radiated pain.

Danek pulled out his phone, scrolled to Amari's name, and pressed the call button.

"Hello?" Amari's sleepy voice answered his call.

"Amari. Adriel's hurt. We're on our way to you." Danek almost barked the words.

"What happened? How bad is he? Shouldn't you take him to my mom?" She sounded panicked, triggering all his protective instincts.

Danek made certain to calm his tone. "I think the hunters who were at the bar attacked us. Adriel was shot. He's alive, but he might not make it all the way to the queen."

"Are you okay?" Her tone was laced with concern.

Danek did a quick mental check for pain. The familiar burn of a bullet crept up his leg, but he was alive.

"I'm fine," he answered her. "We'll be there in five minutes."

"I'm getting up. I'll be ready."

The metallic scent of Adriel's blood permeated the cab as he raced through the streets toward Amari's house. He wasn't sure if Amari could save her brother. She wasn't the queen yet. He hoped she had enough power and skill without the title. She was also the closest option.

He pulled into the driveway of the yellow brick ranch he had left only a few hours before. Amari stood in her garage with the door open, and he pulled in and parked next to her white Mazda.

She ran around the truck and opened the passenger side door, catching Adriel's head as he lost the support from the door. He coughed weakly in her arms. "Dear goddess," she gasped.

"He's been in and out the whole ride over," Danek said. "How can I help you?"

"There's a blanket on the sofa just inside the door. Grab it so we can get him inside."

Danek scrambled through the garage door and into the finished basement, found the blanket Amari had described and rushed back to her side. He followed Amari's instructions in rolling the blanket halfway, tucking it under one side of Adriel, and gently rolling him onto the makeshift body sling.

"You take the corners at the bottom, and I'll take the top. Wrap them around your hands like this."

Danek knew Amari was a skilled mystic healer, but these skills made him think she also dabbled in modern medicine. Her methods reminded him of the military medics.

They maneuvered through the garage and into the basement carrying Adriel, finally getting him to the sofa, where they carefully positioned him onto his belly.

"He's not conscious, Amari," Danek mentioned, worrying over his friend as she washed her hands in the sink nearby.

She didn't answer but returned quickly with a basin of water and gauze and set up a selection of shiny steel tools next to her healing crystals.

"Tell me what to do." Danek felt helpless.

Her hands visibly trembled as she pulled on latex gloves. "I have to take the bullet out. Cut his shirt for me."

He grabbed a pair of scissors from the tray and cut the back of Adriel's shirt, exposing the wound.

He took a step back, seeing Amari kneeling on the floor next to him in her dark blue silk slip and feeling the fear and raw power she was emanating. He turned his attention back to Adriel.

"Hold him down," Amari ordered and picked up a pair of hemostats.

He blinked hard and pressed down on Adriel's upper back as Amari poured rubbing alcohol over the wound, then slipped her finger into the hole in Adriel's lower back.

"I feel it. Stay with me, brother. Don't leave me," Amari whispered. Her voice shifted as she chanted softly in Lasarian.

He recognized healing phrases in her words.

She eased the hemostats into the wound.

Adriel's body contracted, and he yelled out in pain.

"Keep him still! I've almost got it," Amari commanded.

Danek leaned his body onto Adriel in compliance with her instruction.

She deftly pulled the bullet from her brother, tossed the tools aside, and grabbed small rolls of moistened gauze, packing the wound.

Adriel's body relaxed back into unconsciousness. His lips had lost all color, and his breathing was shallow.

"Is he gonna make it?" Danek felt shaky, and memories of Eela's death threatened to send him into a panic. "What else can I do?"

Amari placed crystals in a line down Adriel's spine and rested her hand on the top of his head. "Don't leave me. I might need your energy. Rest."

Danek stood upright and winced, the pain in his leg intensifying. His slacks were damp with blood.

"Crap," he muttered.

Amari's life spirit had entered the higher realm of consciousness as she worked to heal her brother. Her eyes closed tight, and her voice carried an inhuman cadence as she chanted endlessly over her brother. Her body glowed a bright blue as she poured her healing energy into his body.

Danek collected the hemostats and alcohol from her tray and sat in a chair near the laundry tub. He eased his pants down and got to work extracting the bullet from his thigh. It wasn't his first time, and he doubted it would be the last time bandaging a hole in his body. He rinsed the blood from his pants, hung them to dry, and wearily settled into a recliner to watch over Amari.

Nightmares plagued Danek as he drifted in and out of sleep. He woke with a start, his heart pounding in his chest. It took a minute for him to get his bearings. The watch on his wrist read six o'clock.

Amari still knelt on the floor at Adriel's side, and her body faltered as she weakened.

"Danek," she called to him. "I need you."

He came off the chair and stood next to her.

She whispered, "Put your hands on me."

He swallowed hard, his mind flashing back to the last time someone said that to him. His beloved Eela... She still wouldn't allow him peace.

He had rescued Eela from the human lab where they had imprisoned her. She'd said the same words to him that Amari had just whispered, begging him to relieve her pain. He had tried. Fuck, how he'd tried. Eela's once beautiful and healthy body lay bruised, broken, and unfamiliar in his arms, her energy a gray cloud around her. The pain in her voice seared into his brain. She had begged him to save her, pleaded for his energy. He'd poured all his soul, the best he knew how, into her and took her to the queen as fast as he could. She died in his arms that night, and it changed him.

"Danek." Amari raised her head, tears pooling in her bright blue eyes that mirrored the grief in his soul. "Use your pain. Give it all to me, your good and your bad. But you have to touch me so I can use it for Adriel. I need your energy." She panted heavily and looked so pale.

She needed him.

Danek rested his palm on Amari's shoulder. He took a deep breath and lowered mental barriers against his empathic abilities. She gasped when he connected his soul to hers. He grunted, his eyelids snapped open wide, and he dropped to his knees with the sudden intensity of their connection. Passion rippled through him. Blue and gold energies swirled together as their souls blended. Their powerful union gave Amari the strength to stabilize Adriel within the hour.

When the sun's early rays sparkled through the windows, Amari broke her connection to Adriel, and Danek collected her in his arms as she collapsed. Adriel hadn't regained consciousness, but his chest rose and fell normally, and the dressings were dry.

"I think he's going to be okay. Thank you, Danek," Amari

murmured.

Danek held her where she was, both still sitting on the floor in front of the sofa and covered in Adriel's blood. Exhaustion hit him like a freight train. "Thank you, goddess."

Sweat glistened on Amari's skin, and her eyes closed gently. Realization settled over him that Eela was gone, and now his soul needed Amari.

He carried her to the recliner, and she was asleep in his arms before he sat down.

Holding her against him, he closed his eyes. Thoughts of love, new goals, of bettering himself replaced his usual guilt and loneliness. A peaceful feeling settled over him, knowing that Adriel was breathing and Amari was in his arms. It wasn't long before sleep overcame him, and he surrendered to it blissfully.

CHAPTER FOUR

The pounding in Danek's head woke him. He shifted and subsequently groaned in pain.

"Don't move, you dolt," Amari mumbled, sounding sleepy.

He looked down at her in his arms. She lay with total abandon, a bare leg sprawled over the chair's arm, her blonde hair tousled and draped over his arm with her head against his shoulder. Her soul energy drifted around her in a gray fog, depleted from healing her brother.

He would have laughed at her comment if his head didn't hurt so much. His body and brain felt like he had been battling for his life. He reached underneath her bottom, nestled in his lap, and adjusted his erection. "I didn't know."

"Didn't know what?" Amari murmured against his chest.

Danek studied the female in his arms, his gut tightening with renewed pride for his people and sheer awe of his princess. "I didn't know what it took to heal someone. You're amazing."

He felt Amari's soul bonding with him. Waves of her blue energy now clung to his for all to see. It was an honor that she had chosen him. After what they had shared through the night, he could not deny that they worked well together, that he had something to offer her. Her butter-soft blonde hair blanketed his arm, and he twirled a silken lock in his fingers and hugged her closer.

"Stop that," Amari whispered.

"Stop what, darling?"

"Emanating your need. I'm way too exhausted."

He frowned. "I'm sorry." He looked over at Adriel, happy to see his chest rising and falling with quiet, easy breaths. His priority needed to be Amari. "Let's wash up. Where's the bathroom?"

"Up the stairs, second door on the right."

She didn't protest when he scooped her into his arms and carried her up to the bathtub. As the water filled the tub, she sighed deeply. Concerned, he looked deeply into her eyes.

She gave him a warm, reassuring smile. "I'm fine, Danek. Are you okay?"

He nodded and tested the water. "I'm fine. Just a scratch. Maybe you should call your mother and have her check you out." Satisfied with the bath, he turned off the spigot and stood to leave.

She slipped the string of her gown off her delicate shoulder and sighed again. "You're right. I'll call her once I'm clean. There's a pair of Adriel's sweats in the bottom drawer of my dresser. Though you do look hot in your boxers."

Danek felt his face flush. "Thanks, hon. Enjoy your bath." Danek closed the door gently.

Once Amari finished her bath, Danek took his turn. The hot water cascaded over his body, hues of red turning pink and then clear as the blood washed away. He stood in the shower for a long time, the burdens of pain and guilt he carried plaguing his mind. It was past time to fix himself and his reputation. The hunters were getting bold, and the Lasarians would need every available body to fight. Hiding in a bar was no longer an option. It was time to fight again.

He also wanted to move forward with Amari. Her parents needed to know his intentions for their daughter. They might be more receptive if he went to them before they found out from someone else.

Danek peered into her bedroom to check on her. Finding

her bed empty, he descended the stairs to the basement and found her with a basin of soapy water, washing the blood off her brother. He stood back for a moment, admiring her as she worked. Her movements were slow and forced, evidence of her exhaustion, but she still powered through to see Adriel's needs taken care of first. Weaved into her blue aura were waves of his golden energy that clung to her from their combined effort to heal Adriel.

Amari covered Adriel with a blanket and kissed his cheek before standing.

Danek went to her and took the basin from her hands, turning to place it on the end table. "Did you call your mother?"

"Yeah. She wanted to come, but I said I've got it handled." She yawned.

"Go up to bed, Amari. You need to rest. I'll take care of this."

His princess looked at him with a sad frown marring her pretty face. She placed the bloody cloth in the basin and stared at the red water. "You both could have been killed," she whispered. "Is there no safe place for us?"

Danek sighed. "Amari, the humans hunt and kill each other as well as us. Rage is part of their culture. There's been less death since we learned more about humanity and improved our defenses, but I agree that even one death is too many."

"I think about Lasaria a lot. Do you think it would have been safer to stay there with the enemy we knew?" she asked.

"I don't know, darlin'. We don't know what happened to our world after we left it." He rubbed his thumb back and forth on her shoulder, transferring more of his energy.

"I hope we can go back someday," Amari murmured. She moved closer and leaned against him.

Danek encircled her in a comforting embrace, tenderly kissed the top of her head, then repeated his earlier suggestion. "Why don't you go upstairs and get some rest."

"All right," she answered sweetly and turned from him to climb the stairs.

He watched her go and got to work cleaning up. As he rinsed out the basin in the laundry tub and started the wash with all the towels and bloody clothes, he rehearsed his plan in his mind. He would petition the Sirak to resume an active role in the military. As a ranking officer, he could restore his confidence and reputation as well as actively hunt down the human hunters. If his princess felt unsafe, it was his — and every man's — duty to fix it.

CHAPTER FIVE

Am I ready to love someone else? The thought ran through Danek's mind while he brewed coffee in Amari's kitchen the next morning. He could easily fall in love with Amari and wasn't about to leave her side that day in case she or Adriel needed him.

Adriel hadn't regained consciousness, and Danek didn't feel comfortable leaving Amari alone with her brother's status still unknown. They had taken shifts watching Adriel to be sure his wound didn't start to hemorrhage. Amari slept longer hours, but he was willing to give her whatever time she needed. He descended the stairs for his shift, sipping his fresh hot coffee.

He had just sat down after waving Amari upstairs when Adriel groaned, the first sound he'd made in twenty-four hours. He got to his feet and dropped to one knee next to his friend. "Hey buddy, you okay?"

"Someone shot me," Adriel slurred against the pillow.

"Yeah, kinda. You took a bad hit. How're you feeling now?"

Adriel tried to shift his body, only succeeding in breaking out in a sweat. "I feel like shit. Where are we?"

"Amari's."

Adriel's eyes opened, and concern spread across his face. "Where is my sister?"

"She's all right, sleeping at the moment."

Adriel narrowed his gaze. "Amari's blue energy is all over you. What did you do?"

"We saved your life. That's all that really needs to be said right now. I'm going to get you some water and tell your sister you're awake." Danek stood and climbed the stairs to Amari's room.

He sat down gently on the bed beside her and stroked her hair. "Honey."

Amari stirred and opened her eyes, a small smile gracing her lips. "I'm up. Is everything okay?"

"Yeah, your brother's awake. He's talking."

Tears welled in her eyes, and she sniffed. "Thanks, Dan. I'll be right down."

"Are you all right?" He took her hand in his.

She nodded. "Yeah, I'm so happy Adriel's gonna be okay. I feel like I've been walking around in a daze. I can't believe we did that."

He gave her a big smile and kissed her hand. "*You* healed him, Princess. And you were awesome at it. Whenever you're ready, there's fresh coffee."

She smiled back at him broadly. "My hero!"

Danek chuckled and left her room, his next stop being the kitchen, where he fixed a scrambled egg and poured a glass of water for his wounded friend. He balanced the plate on his wrist and carried water and coffee down the stairs. With a great deal of effort, Danek helped Adriel position himself to eat.

"Thanks, man." Adriel took a swig of water. "What is today?"

"November twenty-fifth. It's Tuesday." Danek took a sip of his coffee.

"Where's Amari?" Adriel stared at him for a long moment. "You've taken care of her?"

Danek swallowed and met Adriel's gaze steadily. "Yes. Yes, I did. She needed me to save your life. She'll be down soon."

Adriel forked eggs into his mouth, chewed, and swallowed. "How bad was I?" he asked in a casual tone.

"I'll let her tell you that. I'm no healer. I just did what she asked."

"You have no choice but to complete the bond now and wed her." Adriel's voice turned flat and stern. "You know that."

Danek sighed. He didn't want to have this discussion now. He knew Adriel was unhappy that Amari began to bond with him. There wasn't a man in existence Adriel would deem acceptable for his sister. "I know what I want and what I need to do. I just need time. Besides, there was no other choice. I could not let you die. You are my closest friend and part of the last bloodline of healers."

"Do you love her?" Adriel asked.

"You and I know that you can't truly love another until completely bonded and mated. The connection between Amari and me is stronger than I had with Eela." Danek stared into his coffee when Eela's name fell bittersweet from his lips.

"While Amari may be a closer match to your soul, you have to release what you hold of Eela for it to work," Adriel advised.

"I know that." Danek pulled himself together and changed the subject. "Amari asked me about Lasaria. Is going back even an option?"

Adriel shrugged. "Anything's an option. Not sure if we will see it. Can't hurt to dream about it and have hope."

"We don't have the glass for a Soul Mirror," Danek said.

"Could you make one if the Earthens found the right stuff?" Adriel inquired.

As a Glasser, Danek could manipulate glass, but to make a Soul Mirror, several Magiks needed to come together. Earthens had Land Magik, including power over trees, soil, rocks, and precious stones. To create Soul Mirrors, Glassers needed sand that only an Earthen could conjure.

"I probably could, but I know Kiell could. He made most of them on Lasaria." Danek pondered the idea. With a Soul Mirror, he could take Amari home or wherever they desired. As he finished his coffee, he wondered about their home-world and what it must have been like to live there. A brief fantasy played in his mind of stepping through a Soul Mirror with Amari's hand in his, together seeing Lasaria for the first time and building a home among their people.

His earlier plan started to solidify. Kiell, their chieftain, commander, and fellow Glasser, could restore his military rank. He could also answer his questions about Soul Mirrors. "Adriel, I need to see your parents."

Adriel nodded and chewed. "Yeah, I would say you do. They aren't going to be happy with you."

"What? A mostly grown male Glasser who owns a bar and still holds onto the mate he let get captured and killed isn't acceptable to bond and mate with the heiress to the most powerful Lasarian bloodline?" Danek said with a healthy dose of sarcasm.

"I wouldn't lead with that, no." Adriel smiled.

"Wouldn't lead with what?" Amari stood at the bottom of the stairs.

Danek stood when he heard her voice. Her presence set him on his heels. "You look amazing."

She had showered, and the smell of lilies wafted through the room. The tendrils of her wet hair lay on the curve of her breast. She wore a blue tank and grey sweats that hung low on her hips.

She smiled at him. "Thanks, Danek. Thank you for making coffee." She took another swallow, proving her appreciation. "What are you boys talking about?"

Adriel set his plate down after finishing his breakfast. "We were talking about going back to Lasaria."

Danek's gaze never left Amari. He felt the intensity in her soul at the mention of Lasaria.

"Who brought this up?" Amari shot him a pointed look.

"Danek wanted to know the likelihood of going back to Lasaria," Adriel answered.

"Do you think it's possible, Adriel?" Amari asked.

Adriel shrugged. "Not sure. I don't think we'd be any safer on Lasaria, though. And it might be damaged beyond use for us. There's no way to know what lives there now."

Danek felt Amari's fear rise through their empathic connection. "We could talk about it with your parents. I'm sure they've thought about going back." He consciously filled his thoughts and soul with comfort and peace, knowing Amari was feeding off his emotions as he was hers.

He received a look of gratitude from her. He could be a better man for her. He had a plan. Now he just needed to talk to her parents. "Adriel, are you feeling well enough to go see Kiell? We should tell them what happened."

Adriel swallowed the last of his water. "Get me a refill, and I'll be good to go."

"Whoa, hold on, Adriel. Let me check and dress your wound, and I'll let you know if you're okay to go," Amari scolded. "Danek, get me the gauze and saline from the cabinet." She settled herself on her knees next to the sofa.

Danek returned with the requested items and set them out for her.

She slipped gloves on, waited for Adriel to turn his back to her, and redressed his wound, clicking her tongue disapprovingly. "You should have taken better care of yourself."

"Don't worry, dear sister. The humans will pay for shooting me in the back. You clearing me to get off the couch?"

Amari scowled and shrugged. "It won't kill you, but I advise you to take it easy for another day."

Adriel cupped his hand against Amari's cheek. "I'm sorry

I scared you."

"You almost died, Addy. If Danek hadn't been here, I wouldn't have been able to save you. I can't lose you," Amari professed. "But I know you won't listen, and you're gonna do what you want."

"I'm just going to our parents. I'll be fine. Will you get me a shirt?"

Amari squeezed her brother's hand and stood. She turned and gave Danek a look that melted his heart, then retreated up the stairs. Amari loved without restraint, without pause. These were good qualities for a healer but would make her vulnerable as a queen.

Danek collected Adriel's empty glass. "I drove your truck here. Drop me off at my car, and I'll meet you at your parents' after I stop at my place and change. That's if you're okay to drive?"

"Sure. And hey, thanks."

"Yep, anytime," Danek replied and held out his arm toward Adriel.

His friend gripped his arm in a brotherly gesture and smiled.

"I'll just go get your water before my heart melts," Danek quipped.

"Ha, ha. I'll be right here." Adriel winced as he shifted.

Danek left the basement to fetch Adriel's water. He found Amari standing in the kitchen, staring out the window, a mug of coffee in her hand.

He pressed his body against her side, kissed her cheek gently, and whispered in her ear, "Are you certain you're okay, love?"

She rested her head on his shoulder, and her arm slipped around his waist. "Mmm. Yeah, I'm okay. Thank you."

His soul registered her arousal from contact with his body. He dared not let his mental shields down before he told her how he felt. "We need to talk."

Now that she had rested and her senses seemed intact, they needed to talk about what had happened between them when they had healed Adriel. He wanted to explain his pain and grief and what he felt he had to do for a future with her. He needed to tell her he was ready to move forward.

"What do you want to talk about?" Amari's hand slid up his back gently as she moved behind him.

He let his neck relax, and his head hung forward as her strong hands massaged his muscles. All intelligent thought slipped away. He let her touch him until the ache in his groin became too much to bear. He turned swiftly and backed her against the refrigerator, pressing his body against hers as his lips captured her mouth. She moaned into his kiss and pulled him tighter against her, grinding herself on his erection.

Danek held her close as his mouth traveled down her throat, and his teeth grazed her neck. Christ, this female was so close to coming apart in his arms. Somehow, his brain functioned for a moment, telling him to stop. He suspected her soul was hungry, craving the restorative energy he could offer. He wasn't about to have her for superficial reasons. Now was not the time to claim Amari's body. He fully intended to carry out his plan to be a worthy male for her, and then he could complete their bonding.

He panted against her lips. "Baby, we have to stop. There's a better time for this." He wrapped his arms around her and held her.

She bunched his shirt in her fists and looked up at him. "I know. I can't wait to explore what we can do together. Whatever you need to do, get it done, so you're free to be with me."

"Amari, you are perfection. And I'll be damned if I don't offer you a perfect mate." He cradled her head against his chest and rested his cheek on the top of her head. "I won't come to you any less than a whole partner." *I hope you forgive me for what I have to do.*

There was a chance his plan would hurt her and she wouldn't forgive him. Hell, her brother might kill him before he even got a chance to see her. Still, he had to be honest with her. "I'm going to ask your father to restore my rank in the Sirak."

A captain in the Sirak was often charged with dangerous missions to protect their people. There wasn't a lot of room for a personal life. He would have to leave Amari for an undetermined period. But it was a sure way to release Eela from his soul and give him status as a suitable mate for the princess and a leader of the Lasarian people.

Danek leaned back and searched Amari's gaze. The emotions in her soul were plentiful. All he could do was kiss her hard and wordlessly let her know how much he cared for her, how deeply he valued and respected her, and what he was willing to do for her.

"Please try and understand what I have to do, Amari. I will always come back to you."

"I will hold you to that promise. Don't let me down," she stated with force.

"I understand, Princess. Thank you. I'll pour you another cup of coffee, and then I'm going with Adriel to see Kiell."

Chapter Six

Danek eased his car into the queen's driveway. Her home wasn't a palace by any means but rather a modern colonial house. He parked behind Adriel's truck, got out, and started up the walkway.

Adriel stepped out of his truck and slowly joined him. "Hey, I just got here. How long's it been since you've been here?"

"Five years, give or take." Danek looked up at the house again. The last time he'd been in this house, Kiell had practically carried him. Eela had just died, and he no longer wanted his life to continue, but Kiell had insisted on taking him to the queen for healing.

Adriel nodded. "Well, you're here for a different reason now. Focus on that."

Danek followed Adriel into the house, focusing on Amari and what he must do to be worthy of her.

They entered the sunroom to find Chieftain Kiell and Queen Arrah sitting at the table, Kiell sipping a mojito, Arrah flipping a page in her book. The couple looked up to greet them, and Kiell set his drink down. Arrah sat back in her chair, clearly holding her breath as her gaze scanned Danek.

Danek knew he looked presentable, wearing his black sport coat over a crisp white shirt and black slacks, the traditional colors of the Glasser. Since Kiell was also a Glasser, Danek hoped to gain some favor. If Kiell considered himself suitable for a queen, then Danek figured he should also be acceptable. He stuffed that argument into his back pocket for confidence. There would be no limits to his quest to be Amari's man. Kiell and Arrah's good graces would be a bonus but not completely necessary.

The queen and her chieftain often took their lunch in the expansive sunroom with a vaulted ceiling and enormous stained-glass windows. Sunlight filtered in through the floor-to-ceiling windows, making the queen appear to glow.

Adriel stumbled slightly as they crossed the room, still visibly weak from his injury. Amari had performed nothing short of a miracle to heal him, and Danek worried about what lengths she would go to for her brother.

His gaze shifted to the queen and chieftain, who watched him with unreadable expressions. Kiell got to his feet. The Lasarian chieftain stood six and a half feet tall, two hundred and seventy pounds or so, Danek figured. His heavily muscled body was evident under his clothes. He had dark eyes and wore his hair cut short. Any other time Danek had seen Kiell, his hair had been slicked back with some type of gel. Kiell looked casual this morning, making Danek feel somewhat more comfortable, as he was practically wearing their daughter's soul by now.

"Good morning, Adriel," Kiell addressed his son, then turned to him. "Danek."

"Good morning, sir, goddess." Danek bowed at the waist.

Kiell remained standing, scowling at him. "Breathe, Arrah," he whispered to his mate, audible enough to be heard.

Arrah stood and gracefully crossed the distance to her son. "Adriel," she said in a hushed tone as she took his face between her hands. Her long, gold-painted nails accented her perfectly smooth skin.

"Mom, relax. I'm okay." Adriel pulled away from Arrah and sat, pouring himself a mojito from the pitcher.

Danek remained on his feet, across the table from Kiell, proudly wearing Amari's soul bound to his. Kiell simply stared at him.

Arrah spoke first. "What are your intentions, Danek?"

Wow. She is cutting right to the chase. "Goddess, I am a compatible mate for Amari, and I believe we are full soul mates. I intend to claim, love, and wed her." Danek addressed Arrah with confidence.

Arrah returned to her seat, crossing her arms and looking unimpressed.

Kiell glanced at his wife and turned back to him. "Danek, we recognize your compatibility, it's obvious. However, we still see Eela."

Danek cleared his throat. "I understand that, sir, but I have a plan. I want my rank as captain of the Sirak reinstated."

Adriel coughed on his drink and exclaimed, "You said what? Danek, we got out. Don't get back in."

Danek cast his friend a look and returned his attention to Kiell.

"Sit, Danek. Have a drink," Kiell offered, sinking back onto his chair.

Danek took the seat across from Kiell as the man poured him a drink.

Adriel cleared his throat. "Dad, while you're thinking about Danek's dumbass statement, I have something else you're going to be unhappy about. When we were attacked outside Villa, I had no warning. The humans were somehow able to hide their auras from both of us. Neither one of us detected anything abnormal."

Kiell's scowl deepened. "Who attacked you exactly?"

"Well, I didn't see them *exactly*." Adriel shrugged. "There were hunters in the bar. It's possible a Lasarian may be involved, if they are hiding themselves from us that well."

Danek thought about it. "Adriel's right. Nothing felt off about the hunters. It's possible that the hunters learned something new or are receiving help from a Lasarian." They hadn't detected anything malicious from the hunters in the bar, and the ability to hide emotions was leaps and bounds from what they knew of current human capability.

"That's a serious accusation." Arrah folded her napkin and placed it on the table. "If you weren't my flesh and blood, Adriel, I would take unforgivable offense. You cannot accuse one of our species of trying to kill their own."

Adriel set his glass down hard. "Mother, you can't keep your head in the sand. Look around you! The longer we are on Earth, the more corrupt our people become. It's absolutely possible for us to commit crimes."

"What would you have me do, Adriel? Our people are a small community now. Imprisonment or execution further reduces our numbers," Arrah argued.

"You'd rather leave criminals among us than enforce our laws? If you keep doing that, our community will fall apart anyway," Adriel replied.

Kiell sighed. "Adriel, I agree with your mother, it was late, and you were under duress. Let *us* worry about what to enforce. Stay out of it. Your job right now is to protect your sister."

Danek spoke up for Adriel. "Lasarian corruption is at least worth looking into. A smaller but loyal community is stronger than a larger, broken one. We wouldn't want to be caught with our pants down."

Kiell narrowed his eyes in Danek's direction and nearly snarled, "Your pants need to stay up," then he turned to Adriel. "Has anything else besides your…intuition… led you to believe there's Lasarian involvement with the hunters?"

"We weren't prepared and unable to search the area. Danek barely found me in time, and we got out of there in a hurry," Adriel admitted.

"How badly were you hurt? Amari was pretty vague over the phone." Arrah leaned forward, covered Adriel's hands, and closed her eyes to read his energy. She gasped. "Adriel. You were so close to death. Amari's energy is still strong inside you. Where is she?"

"Amari will be fine," Danek interjected. "She is recovering at home." He was feeling incredibly possessive and protective. It was obvious they were judging him.

Kiell had been his commander and insisted that his soldiers follow certain rules of conduct. At the top of the list was protecting your family. He had failed to do that once—a dreadful mistake he didn't intend to repeat. Amari belonged at his side, and what their species thought of their princess was important to him. He needed his rank and his status back to enforce that.

Arrah's eyebrows rose high in response to his comment, but she turned back to Adriel. "How was she able to bring you back from near death?"

"She had me," Danek answered.

Adriel tried to diffuse the tension. "Amari and Danek used their connection to save my life."

Arrah narrowed her eyes. "Mm-hm. That would explain the extent of her soul bound to you, Danek. Tell Amari I want to see her. It is not an option."

Danek wondered if the Queen's power could end life as well as save it. "She is resting at home, but I'll tell her."

Kiell and Arrah shared a steady look, and Kiell turned back to him. "Danek Kavarac, you provided aide to both Adriel and Amari. I see that you are bonded to Amari. Do you believe you can protect and serve her in the future?"

"We are compatible mates, and I verbally claim her as mine. I know you see my energy and that Amari is part of me now. I'm not playing games. I will return to the Sirak and ascend to the throne at Amari's side, or I will take her to a place where we can be together in peace." Danek tried his best to remain respectful, but they were testing him. He kept quiet about their focus on his relationship with Amari rather than the Lasarian traitor. But to be fair, he and Adriel had shown up at the queen's home unannounced and presented them with unsavory topics.

From the corner of his eye, he saw Adriel wince and stare hard into his drink.

Arrah's body stilled, and Danek held his breath. When a Lasarian was pushed to extreme emotion, their energy, breath, and even heartbeat stood still for an extended moment.

Fury radiated from Kiell. He stood abruptly and growled, "Danek..."

The queen stood and paced to one of her magnificent windows, the stained glass casting rainbows around her. "There are so few Lasarians. Amari's unique bloodline is not compatible with many males on Earth. Danek, part of your soul is still bound to another. You have already failed to protect a woman in your care. And to make it worse, you come here with accusations that one of us is working with human hunters." She sighed and covered her face with her hands.

"The bond is not complete, Arrah. With time apart, it could be dissolved," Kiell said, glaring hard at Danek. "The man has come to us with a plan, but I am not convinced."

Adriel spoke up. "It was Amari who initiated the bond. I trust her judgment. They have a powerful connection already to be able to keep me alive. The humans still hunt us. Putting Danek back in the Sirak and next to Amari will make her safer. And I will always protect her even after she bonds with Danek."

"If Amari chooses to complete this bond, then Danek will become the next chieftain," Arrah snapped as she returned to the table. "Danek, you have been through so much. What happened to Eela was largely out of your control. But how you responded with such crazed grief was weak."

He stared and listened to Arrah respectfully. Her blonde hair framed her face as she looked down at him with the same blue eyes as her daughter.

"Give me my rank and title back, Your Grace. Let me go back to the Sirak so I may become whole again," Danek pleaded.

"I leave this up to you, my love," Kiell said.

Arrah was pensive for several long moments. "I see how this will end. My Magik can't heal everything. I hope that the love from my daughter can restore your soul, Danek. I'll watch you closely." She turned to Kiell and tipped her head to look up at him. "Restore Danek to his rank as captain of the Sirak."

"Approach, Danek, to have your rank restored," Kiell commanded.

Danek took several of the longest steps of his life to stand before Kiell again and accept his rank back.

Kiell extended his arm towards Danek, and Danek gripped the chieftain's arm in return.

Golden sigils formed on Danek's wrist and slowly appeared up to his elbow.

"I restore your rank as Captain Danek Kavarac of the Sirak," Kiell stated.

Kiell released Danek's arm, closed the distance to his wife and framed her face with his hands. "Danek, with your rank restored, purify your mind and your soul. Let go of Eela. Be strong in your purpose as protector. We will talk again of our blessing for you to wed Amari." He wrapped his arm around Arrah, pulled her close, and kissed her soundly. He ran his thumb across her lips, damp from his kiss, gazing lovingly into her eyes.

Danek wanted a love like theirs. Kiell didn't have to explain his actions. He responded to Arrah's need and gave her balance. They were beautiful together. Inseparable blue and gold energies surrounded their forms, linked together for eternity.

"Thank you," Danek said. "For her future, I'll do whatever I need to."

Arrah leaned into Kiell's embrace, bunched his shirt in her fingers, and whispered, "They are both gonna hurt like hell."

Adriel finished his mojito and stood. "Well then, now that's settled, maybe we can research the possibility of a traitor."

Arrah turned her head, still resting on Kiell's chest. "Maybe it's not a traitor, but a Lasarian forced to participate against their will. That's the age-old circle of the Lasarian. Being exploited for their Magik."

"Perhaps," Adriel agreed. "I think we should still look into it as soon as possible. I'll see you both later." Adriel hugged his mother goodbye.

"Don't forget to tell Amari to come see me," Arrah reminded.

Danek stood and bowed slightly toward his queen and commander. "I won't forget. Thank you, Your Grace." He turned and followed Adriel out.

When they reached the porch, Adriel took a deep breath. "I wanna go find these hunters and see what's going on. It was so strange that we felt nothing from them at the bar."

"I can go with you, if you're feeling up to it. I wasn't doing anything this evening. Karai's gonna cover the bar again tonight. We can drive through their usual neighborhoods. Maybe something will feel familiar to that night."

"Onward then, Captain Danek Kavarac." Adriel smiled, bowing at the waist with a flourish of his hand.

"Don't be an ass. Let's go. Follow me down there." Danek shook his head, also smiling, and started down the walkway with his friend.

CHAPTER SEVEN

Danek's car rolled to a stop in the gravel near the old mill off Abrigan Boulevard. He peered out the windshield at the aged red brick building. They'd driven through the streets of Toska for well over an hour, following false energy trails, searching for the humans. All the trails led to this place. The mill stood on the river on the farthest reaches of Toska.

He parked his car in a nearby alley and glanced in his rearview mirror when Adriel pulled in behind him. Visions of his friend lying bloodied and unconscious in that truck flashed through his mind. There was no way Adriel was ready for any physical conflict. Their exploits for the night needed to remain observation only.

Danek shifted his gaze to the mill. Bricks, mortar, and rubble littered the ground, as if the abandoned building had succumbed to the elements. The silvery moon hung low in the sky, reflecting off the river.

Adriel got out of his truck and stood next to Danek's window. "Are you really gonna go back to the Sirak?"

"There's no other choice. I need to have a rank or a title to be with Amari. As a ranking soldier in the Sirak, I will command some respect to stand at her side." He closed his eyes and pinched the bridge of his nose, shifting his thoughts to their current situation. "A Lasarian had to be involved that night. What you said makes total sense."

Danek kept his emotions in check and behind strong shields in his mind. Anxiety raged in his brain. Life was changing again. The bond he shared with Amari was still new and uncontrolled, with the possibility she could sense his emotions from any distance.

Adriel sipped his gas station coffee, staring at the mill. "Well, let's go get a closer look."

Danek watched Adriel amble casually toward the mill. Kiell hadn't exactly provided his blessing about the two of them going out and engaging with hunters to find this shadow Lasarian. It reminded him of the adventures he and Adriel had gone on as kids. As young Lasarians, they'd often used their evolving Magik in mischievous ways. Danek used to remold his parents' drinking glasses into flat sheets or balls. His mother had bound his Magik for a month after he had reshaped her favorite perfume bottle.

Danek shut the car off, grabbed his hat, and followed his friend.

Adriel stopped just short of the building and looked around. "You feel that trail? Weird. It feels like Lasarian energy but just not right." Adriel looked at the mill and walked around the corner. "There's a window over there."

Danek grinned and moved close to the window, placing both his palms against the glass. Closing his eyes, he focused on the Magik in his soul and released the leash on his power. The glass warmed under the steady heat of his hands and softened until he could press through it with his fingers. He collected the molten orange glass and formed it into a neat ball.

"Nicely done, brother," Adriel said.

Danek placed the glass ball in the grass, pulled on his leather gloves, checked that his blade was secure in the sheath at his thigh, and vaulted through the window, stifling a grunt as pain shot up his leg from his wound.

Adriel followed, landing next to him. Voices drifted from a room nearby. He and Adriel crouched low and moved stealthily through the shadows toward the voices.

A quick peek around the edge of the doorway showed four

humans drinking beer from long-neck bottles and gorging on pizza and chips.

A lanky man seated at a table in the center of the room set his beer down and cleared his throat. "Viktor sure ain't around much. Whatever he's looking for better be worth it, cuz he sure ain't been helpin' us."

The stocky man lounging in the corner spoke up. "Our job is to capture the Lasaries alive. I ain't crossing Viktor. Let him come around whenever he damn well pleases."

Danek shared a glance with Adriel and shrugged. He tapped his watch, indicating he didn't want to stay too long. His brain started to burn with an odd kind of itch. It buzzed inside his skull, a sure sign he'd been gone from Amari's side for too long. New mates experienced physical discomfort when parted, and their energies could become imbalanced until their bond was complete.

Danek shifted, ready to leave when someone new came through the back door. The fifth stranger was tall and elegant in appearance, with a square jaw and pale blond hair with several thin, shoulder-length braids. The stranger's energy surrounded him in an inky black fog.

This person wasn't a human. His life spirit was too bold, and his eyes too bright. He could pass as Lasarian, but his energy felt ominous, bordering on evil.

Dread settled in Danek's gut. He shared a confused look with Adriel, who shook his head and shrugged, obviously not knowing what this creature was either.

"Hey, Viktor," one of the humans addressed the newcomer. "How's it going?"

Viktor cracked open a beer, took a long drink, then replied in a strong accent, "Same shite, different day."

"Are we running drills later?" a second human asked.

"No. Drill tomorrow. Sundown. Tonight, I hunt alone," Viktor replied in broken English.

Lasarians adapted well and spoke fluent English. Thoughts raced through Danek's mind. Had he come from Lasaria recently? He could be from a family that stayed isolated from the main colony in the city.

More worrisome was the possible confirmation they were witnessing a Lasarian fraternizing with human hunters. From what was said, it sounded like Viktor was training these humans.

Adriel nudged Danek's shoulder and turned to go.

Danek followed him back through the shadows and out the window, glass crunching under his boots as he hit the ground.

"What the hell was that?" Danek asked as they made their way back to the cars.

"High treason," Adriel growled. "Hell, why didn't we just go in there and slaughter them all right there?"

"Because there are five of them, Adriel. Besides, Amari will have your ass if you reopen that wound. We've got no idea what that creature is. You ever see someone with a soul that dark?"

"Nope." Adriel paused at the front end of Danek's car. "We can't go to Kiell without evidence. He didn't authorize us to be here, and he will shut it down if we tell him about a meeting we saw and a conversation we overheard. We need proof that this is treason or a conspiracy. Let's hang out for a bit and see what happens."

Agitation beat against Danek's skull, the itchy buzz getting worse. His entire being was screaming at him to claim the other half of his soul. He rubbed his head, remembering feeling this way with Eela in the early stages of their bond. His bond with Amari was brand new, and the empathic ability between soul mates still required more than a mental connection. It would get easier once he was completely soul bonded with Amari and could reach her over any distance to calm and comfort her energy.

Danek got into his car, and Adriel followed him and sat in the passenger seat. His friend's expression filled with concern, obviously feeling Danek's anxiety.

"You need to call my sister. You've been away from her too long," Adriel said. "You're having trouble controlling your energy."

Danek glanced at him. "How bad can you feel it?"

"You're restless and agitated. It's not the worst, but I'm sure Amari is also feeling it. She hasn't been connected to a man before," Adriel explained.

Danek nodded and dialed Amari's number. She answered on the first ring, and hearing her voice in his ear eased the itchy feeling in his brain.

"Hey, honey, you doing okay?" Danek kept his voice calm, hoping she couldn't sense his emotions over the phone.

"I feel a ton better hearing your voice, Danek. Where are you?" Amari asked.

Danek found himself smiling. This woman truly brought him joy. "Adriel and I are going out tonight. I can come by in the morning."

"How were my parents?"

"We came to an agreement. I'll tell you about it when I see you."

"I'd feel better if I saw you tonight," Amari requested.

Danek glanced at his watch. He could make it happen for her. "Of course, Princess. Come over to my place in about an hour?"

"Yeah, that sounds nice. What's your address?"

Danek rattled off his address and did a mental run-through of the condition of his house. He was fairly certain he'd bought groceries recently and picked up his underwear off the floor.

"I'll see you later, Dan," Amari said.

"Bye, hon."

"Bye."

Danek ended the call and turned to Adriel. "I guess I have a curfew."

Adriel laughed. "Amari gets what she wants on a routine basis. It's entirely possible she would hunt you down if you're gone too long."

Danek sat back, frustrated. "How long do you think this *Viktor* will stay here?" He was worried Amari would actually come to find him. The last place he wanted her to be was with him when he was doing something dangerous. "I don't want her anywhere near whoever that is." He pointed toward the mill.

"Don't worry about Amari. She's twice the huntress you or I will ever be," Adriel said.

Viktor exited the mill half an hour later. The dark energy blended with the shadows in the alley, and Danek almost missed seeing him. He nudged Adriel, who was napping next to him. Adriel shouldn't be here so soon after his injury.

"I'm up," Adriel mumbled.

"Let's go have a chat with this stranger."

CHAPTER EIGHT

Danek strode toward the mill with Adriel close behind. Viktor turned toward them, taking a defensive stance. "Who are you?"

"Depends," Danek replied, "on who you are."

Viktor bowed at the waist. "I am Viktor. It is pleasure to find not one but two Lasarians."

Danek focused on Viktor, seeing his inhuman raven-black spirit oozing around him. He hadn't seen a creature like him before.

Adriel took a step closer to Viktor and drew his sword, a curved scimitar blade, the traditional Lasarian weapon. "What's your business with the humans?"

Viktor shrugged his elegant shoulders, remaining silent.

Adriel's blue energy flared around him as his temper raged in the presence of evil.

Viktor's eyes widened, and he uttered, "Blue Mage, Prince of Lasaria." He took a step toward them.

"Don't engage. There are four hunters inside. You and I both know how bad this could go," Danek reminded his friend as his heart skipped a beat. Icy fear coursed down his spine upon hearing Viktor speak the Kratoan name for Lasarian healers.

What is this man?

Adriel stalked forward despite Danek's warning.

Adriel and Viktor stood at equal heights. They faced each other within hitting distance, neither backing down.

"I see you, Lasarian Prince, brother to the princess, son of the queen," Viktor taunted in a sing-song tone. "You can't hide your witches forever." He bent his knees and flexed his hands.

Danek took his place at Adriel's side. "You won't touch her," he growled.

Viktor laughed maliciously. "We shall see, brethren, we shall see." He stepped out of the shadows and drew a short sword.

Danek drew his sword from the sheath at his hip and spun it over his hand with a practiced touch.

"Get the hell out of here, Adriel," Danek ordered his prince. They'd fought side by side countless times, but Adriel's last injury was still too fresh for this encounter.

Viktor sprung from his crouch and slashed at Danek.

Danek dodged the attack, spun on his feet, and sank his blade into the back of Viktor's thigh, drawing a spray of blood and a yell from his opponent.

Viktor gripped his wound briefly and then looked at the blood on his hand, a sardonic smile spreading across his face. "Nice. Who are you?"

"Captain of the Sirak, guardian of the people," Danek replied and adjusted his grip on his sword. He kept a close eye on Viktor, ready for his next attack. The man appeared to be an aggressive, impatient fighter who preferred to initiate attacks.

Viktor lunged forward, thrusting his sword, this time landing a deep laceration along Danek's upper arm.

The pain didn't register. Adrenaline surged through Danek's blood, numbing him. He stepped carefully in a slow circle planning his next move, moving within reach of Viktor's strike to draw his attack.

Viktor drew his sword back, and when he swung, Danek dropped and rolled to the side. He sprang to his feet and slashed, his blade opening a gash across Viktor's cheek.

Viktor recoiled, holding his face and howling in pain.

Danek dodged forward, pivoted on his heel, and landed a solid kick into Viktor's chest.

Viktor doubled over and stumbled back a few steps. "This isn't over, Captain," he choked out as he hastily retreated into the alley's shadows, disappearing.

"It's over for tonight," Danek muttered and turned back to Adriel.

"Like riding a bike?" Adriel asked.

Danek chuckled and inspected the wound on his arm. "Yeah, came right back to me. Let's get out of here. Maybe someday I'll go to Amari without blood all over me." He rested his hand on Adriel's shoulder, feeling the exhaustion radiating from his friend.

They returned to their vehicles, and Danek propped his elbows on the roof of his car. "That was all sorts of fucked up."

"Viktor's a Kratoan," Adriel said.

Danek glanced at his friend in disbelief. "He's a *what?* Here? How is that possible?"

Adriel ran his hands over his head for a moment, then rubbed his eyes before responding. "I know how it sounds, but it's the only thing that makes sense. His energy is black, the accent is weird, and you heard what he called me."

"You're trying to tell me that a Kratoan traveled to Earth, shifted form, and joined the human hunters?"

"That's the best answer I have," Adriel admitted. "And if there's one Kratoan, a whole army isn't far behind. It sounds like they are looking for a healer."

"Well, that's the worst possible scenario. They can't have my woman."

Adriel stared at him with an unreadable look. "Just go see what my sister wants. Let her stitch you up. I need to get some rest, and you're late." He stepped into his truck. "G'night," he called as he pulled out of the lot.

Danek waved briefly and settled behind the wheel. He took a deep breath and headed toward his princess.

CHAPTER NINE

Danek parked in his driveway next to Amari's car. He smiled when he saw her sitting inside it and got out to greet her.

"You haven't been waiting too long, I hope," he said as he took her hand, helping her out of her vehicle.

"Nope. Just pulled in. Your house is beautiful." She adjusted her purse strap on her shoulder and stood back, crossing her arms as she took in his appearance. "What happened?"

"We ran into an issue, but it's handled for now." He checked his arm again. The bleeding had slowed to an ooze.

Amari sighed and placed her soft hand on his cheek. "Come on. I'll clean you up."

Danek led her into his house and to his kitchen. "I'm gonna shower real quick. There should be something to drink and some food in here." He rustled through the fridge, pulling out random items. "There are some olives…here's some cheese and a little lunchmeat."

Amari raised an eyebrow. "I'm fine, Danek. Go get your shower."

Danek showered faster than the touchless car wash down the street washed his car, eager to return to his woman. He toweled off and pulled on a fresh pair of pants before making his way down the long hallway to the linen closet to collect his first aid kit.

He paused at the bottom of the staircase, and his hungry gaze devoured Amari as she stretched to replace a photograph on the mantle. The fireplace stood cold and dark, as it had for many years.

"Is this your family's home? It really is remarkable." Amari asked and turned her head toward him.

Danek smiled and crossed the distance between them, his bare feet noiseless on the fur rug. "The house was a gift from Queen Arrah to my mother."

"My mother?" Amari questioned. "Why would she do that?"

"I don't know, love. But it's only a house." Danek knew his house was outwardly impressive to others. People had complimented the high ceilings, the black marble floors spanning from wall to wall, and even the stark white lace drapes covering the windows. But it hadn't truly been a home to him since Eela died.

Amari took the first aid kit and smiled. "Have a seat, and I'll bandage your arm." She moved with graceful steps, her blue and white dress hugging her curves as she walked.

Danek stopped at the buffet and poured himself a scotch. "Can I get you a drink?" He enjoyed the domestic feeling Amari's presence in his home gave him.

"Sure, vodka and tonic, if you have any, with lemon."

Danek mixed her drink and sat next to her on the sofa. "I hope this is okay." He handed her the drink and watched her take a sip, focusing on her lips as she kissed the rim of the glass.

"It's fine, thank you." She placed her glass on a coaster and touched the skin around the laceration on his arm. "What did my father have to say?" she asked as she tended his wound.

Danek sipped his scotch before he answered. "He restored my rank as captain in the Sirak. Having a military rank is essential for our future, Amari. We met under an unexpected circumstance, but I believe in us already."

"What makes you believe in us?" she asked as she wrapped

his arm in gauze.

"I felt something awaken in my soul when you walked into my bar. My first instinct was to run from you. I didn't think I could do this again, be in love and depended on. Your soul is vibrant, Amari. You are so beautiful and kind, and I would be a fool to walk away from the connection we share."

She closed her eyes and rested her head on the couch.

"How tired are you, Amari? Do you need more energy from me?" he murmured, his heart laden with concern.

"I am almost one hundred percent, don't worry," she answered without opening her eyes.

The space between them became too much. Danek shifted closer and rested his hand on Amari's chest over her heart, purposely pushing his restoring energy into her soul.

They both held their breath as their souls crashed together, and the leashes on their passion snapped. He pulled his hand away from her as if burnt.

Amari opened her eyes, the whites of her eyes overtaken by blue, evidence of her power rising to the surface. She slipped her hands behind his neck and pulled him closer, kissing him hard and urgently, moving onto his lap.

Rising passion had them both panting with need. Danek slipped his hands under her shirt and traced up her back. He felt his skin heating up as his desires rose and his control over his power faltered. He grunted and pulled back. "Slow down, babe. I don't want to burn you."

"You can't hurt me." She sounded breathless with her reply. "With our souls connected like this, I have enough power to heal and not get hurt." She kissed him hard and rocked her hips on his lap. "Give me your heat, Glasser."

"Amari," he murmured against her lips, his lust raging higher at her demand for his power.

She threw her head back, and he took the invitation to run his tongue down her throat, pulling the ribbon strap of her gown off with his teeth to bare her shoulder. He rested his forehead on her shoulder, taking a steadying breath before kissing the tattoos on her skin.

"I want you, Danek," she half-whispered, half-moaned, then rotated her hips against his erection.

"And I want you, Amari. I want you bound to my soul forever." He dragged his thumbs across her nipples, hungrily watching the flush travel down her neck and chest. Her breasts rose invitingly under his hands, and he sighed when she brought her lips to his neck, licking a warm path up to his ear.

Her hands traced down his chest and unzipped his pants. She reached between them, freeing his cock, and began a slow stroking motion.

"Oh goddess," he moaned. He cupped her smooth ass under her gauzy dress and held on tight.

He enjoyed her touch for several exquisite moments and fought to stay in control of himself. Surrendering, he growled, gripped her hips, and slid her to the floor onto the fur rug. He straddled her hips, trapping her under him, and stared into her eyes as he stripped her of her dress. "You're so goddamn beautiful."

He worshipped her, lying against her, knowing his heat was igniting her body. "You're mine, Amari." He kissed her lips softly. "Mine to protect." He gently bit her shoulder, pressing against her harder. "Mine to love."

She pressed closer against him and sighed. "Shut up and show me, Danek."

He smiled down at her knowingly as he shoved his jeans over his hips and brought her bare thighs around him. "Amari, you were born for me. I can and will bind you to me completely."

She kissed him hard and ground her core against him. His rock-hard erection pressed into her, making him moan at the feel of her wet heat wrapped around him. It had been so long for him, but he wanted to ensure she remembered this night.

He was relentless in pleasing her. His mouth remained locked to hers, trying to drug her with his kisses while his hands caressed every part of her body he could reach.

Amari's body trembled in his hands, and he could sense her losing control. Her energy swirled high, invading his senses, but he would show her just how strong he was.

She groaned with clear exasperation. "Please, Danek," she begged.

He scooped her off the floor, with one knee on the sofa, bracing a foot on the floor, and held her thigh to his hip. He returned his mouth to hers and sank deep within her core. She cried out into the back of his throat and pressed her body into his.

"I need all of you." She surrendered all control to him. Her mental shields fell, and her need hit him hard.

"I'll give you everything you need, honey." He thrust deeper and picked up speed as his body strained against his control. He had never experienced pleasure like having her legs wrapped around his waist and her nails digging into his arms. His mind swam in the scent of her sex and her sweat as he brought pleasure to them both.

Amari's soul drew on his, replacing what she still needed, her body pleading with him to give her more. Her hands traced up his arms and circled his neck, holding him to her. His name was a heady moan from her lips, and he answered her call, filling her mouth with his tongue as his body filled her hot, wet sheath.

"Christ, baby." He laid his forehead on her shoulder, savoring the feel of her surrounding him, unable to contain the love for her growing in his heart.

She moaned again deep in her throat and was coming undone in his arms. He released his control, held her body tight, and in a frenzied pace, brought her to climax. Her pleasured cries echoed through his mind as he took them higher. He buried his cock deep and emptied himself into her, claiming her body.

When he could breathe, he found her lips and kissed her tenderly. Their energies swirled together around them in hues of blue and gold. They were nearly bonded, only needing a Spellbinder to complete the ritual to unite their souls.

Danek nearly groaned at seeing that part of Eela's energy still lingered, and he grimaced at seeing her red aura intermingled with his and Amari's.

He reached out for Amari's mind with his, finding her energy expended. Her eyes were glassy, but a small smile graced her lips.

The princess needed a soulmate, and any doubts in Danek's mind dissipated as he buried his face into the curve of her neck and rested, letting whatever energy she required soak into her soul. He lay over her protectively, stroking her skin, listening to her breathe, savoring the sound of his heart beating in time with hers, until she sighed and whispered his name. Rolling over to his side, he gave her a little space.

She put her arm around his hip, cuddled against him, and kissed his chest. "We're good together," she said, her breath cool against his heated skin.

"Mmhmm," Danek replied. He felt sated and comfortable with his mate in his arms.

He carried her up to his bed. Her blonde hair lay in waves over his burgundy pillows, and he couldn't help running his fingers through it.

"What are you doing running a bar? It's obvious you aren't hurting for cash." Amari opened her eyes and met his gaze. "Why did you step down from the Sirak, Danek?"

Danek grimaced. The memories of his past still hurt. He lay down beside her and drew her to his side.

"I was on a mission for your father in the North Country. My company was tasked with neutralizing a human lab. We gathered intelligence for weeks on the exact location and occupancy of the place. My soldiers were stealthy. Or so I thought." He didn't want to tell her about his former wife. But she deserved to know, if only this once, who she was falling in love with. And by her expression and the way she looked at him and touched him, he knew she was falling in love with him.

Danek took a deep breath and squeezed Amari gently before continuing his story. "I was gone from Toska for weeks. I promised Eela I would come home in time for our bonding anniversary, so I took leave." He swallowed hard and stared at the ceiling. "The chieftain called and summoned me back urgently. We had to intercept dangerous materials from getting into hunters' hands. I was only supposed to be gone for a few days. When I got back to base camp, Eela's mother had left me several messages. She told me Eela hadn't come home from the market. I abandoned my troop and my rank to search for her. I found her two months and four days later, but it was too late. Humans had captured her and held her in some distorted medical center. I carried her to my truck and drove as fast as I could to the queen, but she didn't make it to the house."

Danek took a ragged breath and cleared his throat before continuing. "After she died, I wasn't fit to be a captain. I never went back to my post. I couldn't go back. I violated orders and ignored calls from the chieftain. When Adriel offered me a partnership in the bar, I grasped at it and hid in that bar. Until I met you, Princess."

"What happened to her, Danek?" Amari whispered.

He tightened his arm around her and collected his emotions. Eela was gone, and telling her story wouldn't change that. Memories of that night played through his mind. He'd found her strapped down to a dirty stretcher, her limbs flaccid and her breaths coming way too slow. Her once musical voice was raspy and weak when she pleaded with him to save her. He would have given his life for her, but the sacrifice wouldn't have been enough.

"The humans build labs where they test things they don't understand, including us. The experiments are brutal, and they treat their subjects like animals or worse. I couldn't save her." His voice cracked as he spoke, and he took a deep breath, trying to calm himself, even as tears burned in his eyes.

"I didn't take care of my wife when I had the chance. I failed to protect her as I had vowed. I blamed the Sirak for keeping me from her. But it was my fault," Danek confessed, opening his heart and soul to the woman in his arms.

Amari rested her hand on his chest, and her aura glowed a bright blue as she tapped into her power, sending her healing energy into his frayed soul.

A feeling of peace settled over him.

They lay in silence for a long while, and Danek thought Amari might have fallen asleep.

"How did meeting me change anything?" Amari challenged.

Danek answered without hesitation, "I fell in love with you, Amari. I believe in you and want to be a better man for you." He tipped her chin and kissed her sweetly.

"Goodnight, Princess," he whispered against her lips, cuddled her close against him, and slept a dreamless sleep.

CHAPTER TEN

Danek woke languidly several hours later. It was still dark. And it was time to report to the Sirak.

He got out of bed, careful not to wake Amari, put clean clothes on, then called Adriel. It was five in the morning, but he knew Adriel would be preparing for his morning meditation. The ritual was a mystery to him, but Adriel insisted the focus on his soul helped him feel balanced and in control.

"Hey, D. You all right?" Adriel asked.

"Yeah." Danek glanced over at Amari, sleeping soundly in his bed. His gaze traced the curve of her back. "I have to go back. Amari coming into my life is a sign. I'm a protector, and we need strong leaders more than ever. She is my second chance."

"You're such an ass, Danek. I understand what you're doing, but you don't have to go back to Sirak to protect her. Your hang-ups about being worthy and having a title are just that, *your* hang-ups. Leaving is just dumb. Amari has no idea the level of danger you're putting yourself in, and she might not forgive you."

"Will you explain it to her?" Danek asked.

"What? You didn't tell her last night?"

Danek paused. "I told her a little bit of what happened to Eela."

"You've become such a coward. You have been out of the Sirak too long. You don't remember what they do. You don't remember the torture factories and cages. I stood next to you when we found Eela."

"I remember, Adriel," Danek snapped. "Because I remember is why I have to go back. We have to end this. I won't let darkness like this exist to threaten my woman. Even if it kills me, it won't get her."

Adriel sighed. "Do what you need to do, Danek. I'll stay and deal with my sister's pain that *you* caused. You shouldn't have allowed your relationship to get this far if you planned to do this."

"I could not have controlled what happened between us. I hope she waits for me. But if she doesn't, at least I will be in a position to always ensure her safety. I won't fail in my duty again."

"You're risking a lot by leaving her to go to the Sirak. She may change her mind about you. And I might let her," Adriel warned. "Amari is a goddess and warrior for our people. She needs a man at her side."

Danek felt like he had time. Amari's mother had even said there weren't many compatible mates on Earth.

"I'll be back as soon as I can. Don't doubt that." He paused, then added, "I'm glad you're okay, brother. Stay out of trouble while I'm gone."

"You do what you gotta do, D," Adriel replied. "Be well."

Danek hung up and packed clothes in a bag before heading to the kitchen to make coffee. He considered waking Amari or leaving a letter but changed his mind. There just wasn't a way to put into words what he felt.

Meeting Amari that first night had changed his outlook on life. He felt excited with renewed hope for a better future. He grabbed his coffee and his bag and headed to the garage. He started his car and backed out of the driveway. With a long look back at his house, he said, "I'm coming back, Amari. Wait for me, woman."

He watched the streetlights fly by as he sped down the highway. The sun would crest on the horizon soon and light the way to his future. The Sirak camp existed in an unnamed part of the country, only able to be found by someone who had already been there.

His thoughts circled around the idea of family. Adriel would take care of Amari without a doubt. Resuming his post in the Sirak was an overdue task. He would take back his life and had a new dream to craft a Soul Mirror to take his princess back to Lasaria. He would build her a magnificent palace, and their children's children would live within its walls.

He checked the rearview mirror and studied Eela's chain hanging from it. Taking it down, he held it tight in his fist for a moment before tucking it into the glovebox and saying a silent goodbye to his former wife.

Danek shifted gears and stomped on the gas, driving toward dreams of returning to his new love's arms and the beginning of their new life together.

ABOUT THE AUTHOR

Remi Auguste is a caregiver, mother, author and friend. Writing for two decades, she draws inspiration from her interpretations of the world around her and enjoys transcribing the love and pain of life onto the page.

www.ingramcontent.com/pod-product-compliance
Lightning Source LLC
Chambersburg PA
CBHW071202130626
46555CB00004B/1551